T5-CVR-742

INTERRUPTING COW

and the
WOLF IN SHEEP'S CLOTHING

To the twins—Caroline and Amelia, off on a new adventure
—J. Y.

To Steve Smallman, Hot Pot, Wolf, and Omelette
—J. D.

SIMON SPOTLIGHT
An imprint of Simon & Schuster Children's Publishing Division
1230 Avenue of the Americas, New York, New York 10020
This Simon Spotlight edition August 2023
Text copyright © 2023 by Jane Yolen
Illustrations copyright © 2023 by Joëlle Dreidemy
For information about special discounts for bulk purchases, please contact
Simon & Schuster Special Sales at 1-866-506-1949 or business@simonandschuster.com.
The Simon & Schuster Speakers Bureau can bring authors to your live event. For more information or
to book an event contact the Simon & Schuster Speakers Bureau at 1-866-248-3049 or visit our website
at www.simonspeakers.com.
Manufactured in the United States of America 0723 LAK
10 9 8 7 6 5 4 3 2 1
Library of Congress Cataloging-in-Publication Data
Names: Yolen, Jane, author. | Dreidemy, Joëlle, illustrator.
Title: Interrupting cow and the wolf in sheep's clothing / by Jane Yolen;
illustrated by Joëlle Dreidemy.
Description: Simon Spotlight edition. | New York, New York : Simon Spotlight, [2023] |
Series: Interrupting Cow | Audience: Ages 5 to 7. | Summary: Interrupting Cow introduces a lonely
wolf to her friends, and they all share her famous knock-knock joke.
Identifiers: LCCN 2022050356 (print) | LCCN 2022050357 (ebook) |
ISBN 9781665914437 (hardcover) | ISBN 9781665914420 (paperback) |
ISBN 9781665914444 (ebook)
Subjects: CYAC: Jokes—Fiction. | Cows—Fiction. | Wolves—Fiction. | Friendship—Fiction. |
Humorous stories. | LCGFT: Humorous fiction. | Picture books.
Classification: LCC PZ7.Y78 Is 2023 (print) | LCC PZ7.Y78 (ebook) | DDC [E]—dc23
LC record available at https://lccn.loc.gov/2022050356
LC ebook record available at https://lccn.loc.gov/2022050357

InterRupting COW

and the
Wolf in Sheep's Clothing

by Jane Yolen
illustrated by Joëlle Dreidemy

Ready-to-Read

Simon Spotlight
New York   London   Toronto   Sydney   New Delhi

It was morning, and the cows
were shrieking instead of mooing.
"Monster!" one cried.
"*Moo*-nster!" the others screamed.

Interrupting Cow woke in confusion,
without even time to tell her favorite
knock-knock joke—
the one her friends all liked.

Not her cow friends.
She had no cow friends.
Her other friends.
But that was all right,
because the cows had already run
from the barn, leaving her far behind.

Interrupting Cow looked around and
saw what must be the monster.
Some kind of sheep, she thought.
Its wool was thin and seemed to be
slipping off to one side
of its lean body.

Hoping to comfort the uncomfortable-looking creature, Interrupting Cow began to tell her famous knock-knock joke.

"Knock, knock!" she said *smooooo*thly.

The monster said nothing.

So she answered herself, while moving closer: "Who's there?"

ill nothing.

nterrupting Cow," she said.

he creature barely lifted her head,

nd she said, "Interrupting Cow w—"

MOO!" she shouted.

HOWL!" the creature said at

he same time.

owl *is not a sheep sound,*

hought Interrupting Cow.

Interrupting Cow watched the sheep.
"You are an odd sort of sheep,"
she said. "Perhaps even a very
ba*aaaa*d one."
That joke did not make
the strange sheep laugh either.

Howl," the strange sheep said again.
Baaa-howl."

"I don't like jokes,"
growled the strange sheep.
Growl *is not a sheep sound either*,
thought Interrupting Cow.
"What do you like?"
Interrupting Cow asked.

"Friends," said the strange sheep.
She sounded sad.
"And do you have many?"
Interrupting Cow asked.
The strange sheep shook
her head. "None."

"But sheep go in herds,"
said Interrupting Cow.
"I have no herd. No friends,"
the strange sheep replied.

"Ah, but you have *heard* of them?"
Interrupting Cow thought
that small joke might make
the strange sheep smile.

The strange sheep took a step
toward Interrupting Cow.
"Groan," she said.
Groan *is not a sheep sound.*

But Interrupting Cow was already galloping away, shouting to the strange sheep, "Follow me! I have lots of friends. And you can share!"

As she ran past cows and horses in the meadow, they galloped away from her, shouting, "Run! Run! Run!"

As she passed the ducks
making curlicues in the pond,
they cried out, "Swim! Swim! Swim!"

As she passed the goats
on the tops of their houses,
they screamed, "Climb higher!"

But when at last she saw her herd of friends standing by the roadside, all laughing and waiting for her, she slowed and turned to the strange sheep to introduce them.

The sheep, who was not really a sheep
stood with her head down,
looking miserable.
Her shorn wool coat was now
twisted around her knees.

Huffing and puffing from the run,
she was about to blow herself down.
But instead, she managed to say,
"I don't have any friends because . . ."
She took a big breath.
"Nobody likes a big bad wolf."

"Nonsense!" said Interrupting Cow. "My friends are your friends now." And she introduced the wolf to Who the owl, to the zebra who was black and white but not red all over, to the old dog who now knew new tricks, and to the Rhode Island red rooster who loved crossing roads.

This is our newest friend," she said.
She is a wolf in sheep's clothing.
She needs new tricks and a better
sewing machine. But mostly she needs
a herd of friends."
She smiled at the wolf.
The wolf smiled back.

And then Interrupting Cow chuckled
and added, "Knock, knock."
"Who's there?" all her friends
asked together.
"Interrupting Cow," she said.
Together they asked,
"Interrupting Cow—"
But before they asked who,
the entire herd sang out with
"WHOOOO," "MOOOOO,"
"COCK-A-DOODLE-DOO,"
"NEIGH," and "WOOF."

HOWWLL

And the loudest of all was
the wolf in sheep's clothing's
"HOWWWWWWL,"
which was so loud,
it even brought up the moon.